This book was written by Darren Moore (me) but wouldn't have been possible without the help and support of both Rawlins Academy and Happy Group LTD.

With special thanks to my chief editor, Rachel Yates. My fabulous mentors, Robbie Everitt and Johara Allen. And, of course, my amazing friends, Jackie, Marvin and Alana.

In recognition of the hard work achieved by Rawlins Academy and Happy Group LTD.

"Wake up, Simon!"

Groaning Simon gradually woke up to the sound of his mother's voice.

"Coming Mum. Give me a sec."

"You'll be late." She warned.

"I know, I know."

Grabbing a clean-ish tracksuit from the floor, he grabbed some underwear and ran to the shower. Watching the water cascade down on his head Simon began contemplating his daily routine of being shouted awake followed by a rushed shower and then running to the bus stop. Simon turned the dial to turn off the water. He then sighed. Today they had an Assembly. These occurred once a week, usually on a Wednesday but today was Friday and they were having another.

Running downstairs, Simon could smell the burnt toast. Grabbing a slice as he ran out the door he realised that he had left his bag in his room. Turning around he heard the bus slow down as it neared the bus stop. Cursing his stupidity, he waved at the driver to ask him to wait. He then ran upstairs, slung the bag over his shoulder, and ran outside. He looked at the stop. *Empty.* The bus had left. Looking at his watch, he saw that he was definitely going to be late. Calling Reception, he heard the voice of one of the sympathetic receptionists.

"Hello, Alexander Academy Reception, how can I help?"

"Hi, my name is Simon Greene; I'm a student at the Academy."

"How can I help Simon?"

"I'm running late, Miss. The bus left."

"You really should wake up earlier. Let me just check something on the system."

Simon heard the clacking of the keyboard in front of the receptionist.

"Simon Greene?"

"Yes Miss?"
"According to the system, you have been late twelve times this term. For the same reason you just gave me. Hang on. There is a note here on Sims (the register system). It says here that you have an appointment at 11 and won't be in today."

"Oh. Ok. Thanks Miss."
"No worries, Simon."

The line went dead. Feeling a tap on his shoulder, he turned around and struck with his palm into the person's shoulder. Grunting the large man just smiled.

"My name is Harry Blue. I work for a company that would like to hire you. You will have to go through SAS training and a separate training programme."
"To do what?" Simon exclaimed

"Be a Protection Agent, Or Bodyguard as you may know

them as. You'll be in a CPG, or a Close Protection Group."

"I am only 14, you know. I am too young. Now if you don't mind, I'm going home."

"Your dad worked for us."

Shocked he stopped walking away and turned back.

"*What!* He died seven years ago in a car crash. I went to the funeral!"

"That is why I said *worked*. He died on assignment. He was shot. I can prove it if you want."

"You're telling me that I was lied to my whole life?"

"No, only about your father's job and how he died. On his desk, against regulation I may add, he had as photograph of you and your mother. He loved you both. Here." He passed over a photograph in an ornate brown frame.

Inside Simon recognised his dad. He let out an involuntary gasp. Hand over his mouth, he fell to the floor and began sobbing.

"Your Grandfather started the company. Your Grandmother asked me to offer you the job as Team Leader for a Youth Bodyguard Division or the YBD."

"But she… she has cancer! I sometimes have to help. I can't go to Wales!"

It was Harry's turn to look surprised.

"How do you know SAS training takes place in Wales?"

"My Uncle was in the SAS."

"No he wasn't. Why would you lie? I, we, already know you hacked into the NSA's satellites and the Police System to exonerate your cousin from Drink Driving. In addition, the fact that you hacked your school. Now your Grandmother wants to see you at our Headquarters. If you're up to it?"

"I can leave?"

"Of course. If you wish. Now my car is over here." He pointed to a brand new off-road silver Range Rover with tinted windows. "It's armoured and bulletproof. The tyres are run flat. AI can control the car if the driver is killed. This is a one-off half a million-pound car."

Simon calmly walked to the car as he sensed a third presence. Turning around he saw a slight glare as something glass reflected off the sun. He ran over to Harry and bowled him over as the bullet hit the tarmac where he was stood.

"Christ! Get in the car, Simon! Now!"

Ignoring him, he felt his hip and found the pistol he expected to find.

"No you can't use that Simon, you're not trained!"

Simon rolled off Harry and ran to a nearby tree. He had a slight flashback.

"Son, remember the target moves. This is not archery. Now breathe out, aim and fire."

"I know Dad. Hang on."

Bang. Missed.

"You'll get it eventually. Now behave, yeah? Look after Mum for me while I'm gone."

"I will Dad."

With a tear in his eye, Simon stepped out and breathed gently out to steady his aim. With the gun aimed at the rooftop, he fired. He saw the glass glare again as the gun fell from the roof followed by a man.

Shaking at having killed someone, Simon froze. The man landed on the floor with a thud. Harry ran towards him. But his vision blurred and the last thing he remembered was seeing a blue Jaguar driving towards them.

When he woke, he felt the bump of a car driving off-road.

"Are you ok, Simon?"

"Yes thank you Harry, what happened?"

"I was followed as I came to get you and they tried killing you. Good shot by the way. About two hundred feet away and on a roof.

I have had immense training and I could not make that shot! Anyway, next a Jaguar came up just as you fainted. If you look behind us, they are following. Do not worry they are friendly; they were alerted to the danger when the shot went off. I radioed HQ and they are expecting us. How'd you feel?"

"Fine. My dad... My dad taught me to shoot... I guess... I never knew I'd actually kill someone..." Simon broke down and cried hugging his legs.

"Hey, you listen to me mate. It was him or me *and* you. You did what you had to. But next time you steal my gun, I swear I'll beat you up!"

"No you won't." Simon smiled.

"Look, I know I should be thanking you for your bravery but... That gun was supposed to be unloaded and that sniper was a test to see your response. You passed. However, he died. And he was on our side."

"He was *what?*"

"I know, I'm sorry. It was my fault I should have emptied the gun."

Simon stayed silent. He looked out the window at the roads driving past and the hills passing by too quickly. He recognised a sign written in Welsh. It read 'Private Land, trespassers will be shot.'

Looking around he felt the car slow down near a gate. Three suited men came and searched the car as they escorted Simon into the complex. Three seconds later the car blew up. Harry had turned off the ignition triggering the bomb. Simon felt the heat as it burned and blistered his skin. Screaming he fell as they bowled him to the ground covering him with their bodies. Finally, after what felt like an eternity, they were rolled off him. As Simon was helped to his feet, he could not help but look at the Security Agents burns. He hobbled along with the people who had helped him up towards the front door of the building. Outside the building, a single agent ran forward and grabbed the door. Simon was rushed inside and onto an EvacChair. One of the Security Team pushed the chair-like stretcher. He was rushed into a room marked Private and the door was closed.

Behind an ornate mahogany desk sat his Grandma.

"Grandma? I thought you were in hospital with cancer?"

"Oh, dear. I was and still am. I was let out to see my grandson join his Grandfathers Company. Your father was his first employee. He was so... as proud of him as he... as he will be of you..."

"Grandma, it's ok. You are ok. I am fine. But I don't know anything about this job."

"Well, your grandfather started it twenty years ago with two of his friends. Your father was 15 at the time; he joined and had some specialised training. When he turned 18, he began proper security, training with the SAS, the FBI and MI6. Two years ago, he was assigned with protecting the First Daughter. A group of terrorists took over the convoy, killing both the daughter and your father. Afterwards the Son, being protected by another agent was kidnapped and the President killed himself, you probably know of that story from the news. Truth is the government were asked to be given eight hundred million dollars in exchange for the child. That was when I had the epiphany of hiring younger people to protect the children. Invisible security. A last ring of defence. The US government refused as did our own. That is until, behind their backs, we offered that service. The child had been found homeless at eight. They had trained for 6 years and were as ready as they would ever be. They protected a millionaire's son on a yacht holiday. The yacht was attacked by *thirty* boats. All of the men were killed before they could get to the child. All of the boats security had been compromised. She then drove the boat to a nearby harbour and requested assistance from us. Officially, the government never changed their minds. Unofficially they agreed that this could come in helpful for visiting dignitaries and their children. We want you to join us and go through the training so that in eight months you are ready for being a Team Leader. Are you up for the challenge my boy?"

"Would I be here if I wasn't Grandma?"

"That's Ma'am to you now." She smiled. "Or Mrs Greene. You will be referred to as Alpha Zero by the staff but the kids will call you… Have you chosen a name?"

"Huh?"

"Huh what?"

"Huh, ma'am?"

"Well, you are given a new identity when you join so that you can change your past."

"But I want to stay a Greene."

"You can. But change your first name."

"Ok. Kyle."

"You're sure?"

"Yep."

"Ok then Mr Kyle Greene. You are in Alpha Team. Alpha One is waiting outside. Good luck."

"Thanks Grand... Ma'am."

There was a slight knock at the door.

"Enter." The Commander (Grandma) said.

"Hi, you must be Alpha Zero?" She looked directly at a blank part of the carpet.

"I'm over here." Simon was slightly confused.

"Oh sorry. I am blind. I cannot see you. Have you got any bags with you?"

"I…"

"On their way but its ok Alpha One" The Commander interrupted.

"Yes Commander. What's your name Alpha Zero?"

"Kyle Greene."

"Oh cool. A Greenie." She giggled. "Sorry I'm a fan of Maze Runner. An inside joke. Never mind." She turned around and began leaving the room.

When they'd left the room Alpha One looked around not sure what to do.

"I think I'm going to my room. What's your name by the way?"

"Amelia. This way. I think."

"So how can you be a blind bodyguard?"

She turned around quick as a viper.

"I beg your pardon?"

"I only meant it as though... like... how do you see danger?"

She walked towards him and stopped right in his face. She pushed one finger into his stomach. Feeling extreme agony Simon doubled over. With a swift kick, she connected gently with his head.

"And unconscious. Next thing I call the Police and they provide assistance. I return to my Principle and Job Done. That's how a blind person becomes a bodyguard."

Still in agony, Simon nodded in agreement before saying yes remembering she could not see him.

"I also have a modified earpiece that transmits locations and things through sound. And an automatic glasses scanner searches for danger on a constant basis."

Impressed, Simon was directed into a room near the entrance. Inside the room was four bunk beds, a communal ensuite and a sort of office. On the bunk beds, minus one of the beds, stood seven smartly dressed children.

Amelia walked to a bunk bed around the corner and stood to attention.

"Morning, Sir. Welcome to Alpha Squad Room. Thank you for joining Alpha Team."

Like a robot, all of them said this at once.

Then they walked over one-by-one and introduced themselves.

Connor, the brown haired IT Geek, greeted him first. Then it was Sarah, a blonde haired Agent. Followed swiftly by Adam, a six-foot eight fifteen-year-old monstrosity of an agent. Behind him was Gary, a wheelchair bound Gadget Guy. Amelia reintroduced herself as the blind Agent. Next was Damian, a dwarf Agent. Finally, came Drake, a very muscular seventeen-year-old Comms Officer. Then Simon (Kyle) introduced himself.

"I'm Kyle, the Team Leader when I pass training. Any tips?"

"Sure, don't die." Apparently, Gary was also a comedian.

"How about be cautious. Those SAS guys will chew you up!" Connor clearly knew his stuff.

Eight weeks later

"Alpha Zero to Comms, Alpha Zero to Comms."

"This is Comms. Alpha Two speaking, go ahead."

"Eagle is two yards from destination, over."

"Roger that Alpha Zero."

"Oh god! Shots fired, shots fired. Location, some sort of silo near his house. I repeat a silo near Eagles house."

"Hawk and Sparrow en route to your location. Hang tight. ETA three minutes."

Hawk and Sparrow were the radio names for the Back-up helicopters. Eagle was the Principle (the person being protected.)

Outside the building, a training exercise was taking place with most of Alpha Team. Earlier that month, they had lost a teammate. Adam had been killed sacrificing himself for his Principle outside the hotel in Paris. His family had been told that he was on a school trip when terrorists came to the hotel. Gary was exempt as he was disabled and Connor had broken his arm trying out a handheld machine designed by Gary. Everyone but Drake was outside because he was operating Communications (Comms) for the team.

Three months later.

"Kyle Greene I am proud to bestow upon you the Golden Wings of a Full Agent. Congratulations."

Kyle bowed to the audience.

"And here the Rainbow Team Leader Wings." Another bow.

"And last but not least, you're ID. Welcome to Youth Bodyguard

Division. Alpha Team is now complete and at full operation status. These Blue wings recognise that fact. If Alpha Team could come up the stage." All of them were given the blue wings. Crying in the audience, his Grandma clapped. Next to her was a Police Officer briefed on the existence of the company. Suddenly she convulsed as she had a heart attack.

"Grandma!" Kyle ran down the stage to his grandma.

The Officer tried his best but she was dead.

Crying the rest of Alpha Team comforted him.

Two days later

"... Was a perfect woman. An example of what society should be. I have no doubt that she is on her way to the Pearly Gates. She died young, she was only 67. Thank you for listening."

Crying Kyle finished his funeral speech. Since joining YBD (Young Bodyguard Division) he'd lost eighteen kilos and was now muscular. Now 15 he missed his normal life. In two months he was going on assignment with Alpha Team. He was dreading it. They had two principles, brother and sister. Both were children of Billionaire Alexander 'Alexander the Great' Hopewell.

When Alpha Team returned to Base a man in a navy suit complemented by a white shirt and navy bow tie.

"You must be Alpha Team. My name is Colonel Regale from the US Armed Forces. I've been given the promotion to Young Bodyguard Division Captain. Director Crowe is in the Commanders office. He is now the company superior until you turn eighteen Kyle and then Commander Greene left Greene Security Services to you in her will." Regale saluted and turned on his heels.

Two days after the funeral it was time for Operation Golden Sword to begin.

OPERATION GOLDEN SWORD

MSSION BREIFING FOR ALPHA TEAM

CLASSIFIED

DOCUMENT ID – 778145L45.

TEAM LEADER – KYLE GREENE

OPERATION LEADER – DIRECTOR CROWE, GSS, YBD

COMMUNICATIONS OFFICER – DRAKE MERIN

CLIENT – ALEXANDER HOPEWELL

PRINCIPLE ALPHA ONE – BARTHOLEMEW HOPEWELL

PRINCIPLE ALPHA TWO – SARA HOPWELL

YBD OPERATIVES

ALPHA ONE – KYLE GREENE

ALPHA TWO – AMELIA KINGSTON, LEWIS LOCKE

CLIENT TO EXPLAIN MISSION UPON ARRIVAL TO MANOR D'HOPEWELL, FRANCE, EUROPE.

ALL AGENTS TO SEE GARY AND CONNOR SPERK BEFORE OPERATION BEGINS.

TRANSPORTATION ARRANGED.

This was the short document given to Alpha Team.

"So, what's Plan A?" Kyle began quizzing everyone on the Mission Protocols.

"If anything goes wrong we evacuate our Principles using any vehicle possible but preferably a bullet proof or armoured vehicle. Stick together if possible." Amelia replied.

"And Plan B, Lewis?" Lewis was a new operative.

"Um… Hide and contact HQ to arrange a pick-up. Do not engage the enemy unless absolutely necessary."

"Good. Plan C?"

"Improvise your way out?"
Nobody knew except Connor.

"Good, now, Connor I believe you have Go-Bags for us?"
"Yep. All personalised for each Agent and the situations that may arise during the mission. We have peppermint breath spray, it is actually a stun gun, so be careful. A mobile phone, obviously. Earpieces, sunglasses, armoured clothing as standard. Also this" he produced a bar of chocolate "in case you get hungry on your flight." He grinned.

"What about this?" Lewis pointed to a handheld games console. There were two of them.

"Oh I almost forgot. Your in-flight entertainment. Enjoy."

Alpha Team went their separate ways wishing each other luck on the assignment.

On board the flight, Kyle sat in between Amelia and Lewis. Both were making use of the in-flight entertainment provided by Connor.

"Base to Alpha One, respond."

"This is Alpha One. Over."

"Sit-rep. (situation report)."

"On-flight. Ten minutes from Airport."

"Roger that. Pickup is a black Mercedes Maybach Limousine, license plate H093W311. That's Hotel, Zero, Nine Three, Whiskey, Three, One, One."

"Roger, name of driver?"

"Steven McGuiness. There are also three bodyguards. Look out

for them."
"Thanks for the head-up."
"Oh before you go, Gary wants to speak to you on Channel Eight alone."

Looking at the two in between him, he pondered why Gary wanted to speak to him.

"Just going to the loo, shout if you need me." He hated lying but did not have a choice.

Once in the bathroom he keyed the earpiece to Channel 8.

"Kyle Greene."

"Oh good the message was delivered." The voice did not belong to Gary. Kyle tried placing the voice but could not.

"Who is this?"

He heard a tut on the other end.

"You don't recognise your superior's voice? It's Director Crowe."

"Oh sorry, sir. Why the secrecy?"

"Your operation just went from Code Orange to Code Blue. Alexander's convoy was just hit on its way to the dock. Nobody but you know about this. Use the team. Tell them if you have to or if you think it is appropriate. Beta Team are on standby nearby if you need them. *Under no circumstances is Amelia to partake in this mission.*"

"Sir she can take care of herself."
"Not this time, Kyle. Not a Code Blue. I know you are technically the boss and she's your mate, but... Come on mate. Tell her we have found a better operation with Charlie Team, protecting US President King's daughter. She loves her. Of course the mission

is made up but it'll get her back to HQ."

"Yes, sir."

Leaving Channel 8 and re-joining Channel 1, he heard the anxious voice of his teammates.

"Kyle, respond now dammit!"

"Sorry, Lewis didn't hear my mic."

"Bullshit Kyle! We heard your conversation with the Director!"

"What!"

"I'm sorry but I was suspicious! Code Blue? Is the Director mad?

We *need* three operatives at least!"

"Lewis, calm down. Please. I know our comfortable yacht mission just turned sideways but we can do this. We were trained to."

When they landed Amelia knew to follow orders and stayed aboard for the return trip.

Lewis refused to talk to him until they arrived at the limo.

"Mr McGuiness?"

"How do you know that name young man?"

"I'm Kyle Greene, YBD."

Chuckling the large driver just kept looking at the jet.

"And I'm the Queen! Go to your mammy."

Pulling out his Agent ID the driver finally relented.

"We have a problem Agent Greene. Mr Hopewell and his family have been kidnapped. That means your services are no longer required. Send my regards "to Commander Greene."

"She is dead. My Grandma died a short while ago."

"Then... Who's in charge now?"

"Director Crowe is in charge of Greene Security but Captain Regale is in charge of YBD."

"When I heard the name Young Bodyguard Division I expected 18 – 21 year olds not 14 and 15 year olds! What's England coming to?"

"We do what we have to, to protect our Principles. Until we get confirmation of our Mission

Termination, we will stay here. Take us to the Yacht."
"You mean The Hope of the Sea?"

"Yes, what other Yacht would I be on about?"
"Well, Mr Hopewell has twelve including Hope of the Sea, there's Hope of the Ocean, The Hopewell, The Well-off..."

"Oh, sorry I didn't know he had twelve yachts!"

"It's ok, Agent Greene. Why don't you contact your HQ to confirm the termination of your operation?"

"Comms, this is Alpha One, respond."

"Kyle, run! HQ's been compromised! Threat level Orange! Ugh!" the last noise sounded like Connor had been punched in the gut.

"Listen here Greene. Your Grandfather sends his regards. He is waiting for you in Paris. He is in Hotel d' Paris, room 107. Good luck and welcome to France!"

Shocked Kyle looked at the driver.

"To Hotel Paris, now!"

"What's going on Kyle?" Lewis's earpiece had fallen out on the plane.

"HQ's been attacked! We are rendezvousing at the Hotel. Agent Locke, Beta team Leader is there."

"Ok."

The driver accelerated away from the airport towards the iconic cylindrical Hotel. The driver pulled them right up to the door. Unperturbed by the arrival of a limo, the door attendant opened the rear door and then the hotel door to let the VIP's into the hotel.

Walking to the receptionist Kyle asked for the occupant's name of Room 107.

"That would be Gary Greene, checked in two hours ago."

"Thank you."

Running up the stairs two at a time, he knocked on the door of room 107.

"Come in, Simon. Or should I say Kyle now."

"Granddad?" reluctantly walking in he saw his grandfather laid out on the sofa.

"Not anymore, Kyle. I had to fake my death so that your Grandma would hire you, my dying wish. Greene Security went bankrupt three years ago Kyle. The funding is now completely dried up. I had to stage an attack to claim the insurance. By now, everyone on-site will be dead. Oh, and by the way, Alexander Hopewell does not exist. He's one of my more successful fake ID's."

"You staged an attack on the most prized possession of the Greene family and Legacy? I am ashamed to say that you are related to me. Goodbye, Gary." Emphasizing the use of his first name showed the refusal from his grandson.

"Kyle, please! I'm sorry!"

"No you're not! You're only sorry that you have no money left!" Kyle turned around for a final look at his grandfather before spitting on the ground clearly showing the barrier now created between them.

Going back downstairs, Kyle had to fight off the tears as Lewis met him halfway up.

"I just asked reception, Agent Locke isn't here, none of his fake ID's have checked in. Who did you really come to see?"

"My… My… grandfather…"

"The one who started Greene Security? He's dead."

"No he faked his death. GSS went bankrupt three years ago and now the fund he set up is running dry, so he staged an attack on HQ... and ordered... the execution of everyone on-site..."

"Oh my god! That's awful!"

"Let us go... before he comes out and kills us both. I recorded our conversation with my phone. If we can get it to the Police..."

"You're going to turn in your own blood?"

"He was going to *kill* his! He deserves every single minute he gets in a cell!" going from tearful to angry Kyle simply carried on walking to the limo.

Realising his Team Leader had been emotionally compromised; Lewis knew he had to find a way of taking over control of the mission before everything went wrong.

"Kyle... Maybe I should take charge, you know until you regain your emotions?"

"Definitely not! I'm Team Leader not you." He broke down again. "I'm sorry. I am so sorry. They are all dead. Because of my family name!"

"No, in no way is this your fault! Everyone is dead because your Grandfather is a dirty, dirty bastard. He started the company, and then he chose to end it. Well, guess what? I didn't hear anyone terminate the mission so as far as I'm concerned we have a job to do."

"You're right, Lewis but... My Grandfather is Mr Hopewell; none of our principles actually exist."

4 YEARS LATER.

"All agents Status Report." Having turned 18, Kyle was now in charge of Greene Security and in turn the YBD. The attack had resulted in all 50 trillion pounds of insurance going into limbo until Kyle turned 18. He ensured that his Grandfather saw not a penny of it.

Unfortunately, after the attack all of the YBD Agents had refused to return.

"This is YBD Team Delta; all is good, at Threat Level Green. Over."

"Roger that, YBD Delta. Continue as normal. Out."

"This is YBD Team Alpha, all good, Threat Level Green. Out."

"This is YBD Team hotel; all is not good. Threat Level Red, Principles Alpha One and Two have vanished from Location Golf Eight. Please advice, over."

"This is Director Greene, sending GS Alpha to assist in the search, expect a black Humvee."

A new security measure designed and maintained by Kyle meant that an 'adult' security team were on hand.

"This is GS Alpha, licence plate GS ONE is two minutes out, two minutes out over."

"Engaging direct Comms to YBD Hotel, GS Alpha, out."

In a black armoured Humvee, Agent Lewis Locke drove with precision right to the gated entrance to the community zone where Team Hotel's principle, Alex Manchez lived. Showing his badge persuaded the Gate security officer to open the gates.

Driving the regulation 15mph Lewis was talking to his team, preparing them for the mission ahead.

"Right, so we have two missing principles. They went missing from their bedrooms, which means we have no idea, what they are wearing. What we do know is that this is not typical of these principles. One is Mr Manchez, our client; the other is

Miss Elizabeth Manchez, our client's daughter, any questions?"

"Yeah how did YBD lose both people?" Agent Smith asked.

There were a few chuckles in the car.

"Well, Agent Locke, it's because unlike you, they're human. As are both clients. Sometimes they vanish and then return like that time you put your team on Code Blue when your client went to the corner shop for milk. Remember that? It is why you are here, demoted. It has nothing to do with experience or stupidity, got it?"

"Yes, sir. I just meant... Never mind."

"Sir, with all due respect, isn't Director Greene a bit young to be giving orders? Colonel Kingston is old enough to be his granddad."

"No, Colonel Kingston is not a dickhead, unlike Director Greene's actual Grandfather."

"You know the Founder?"

"Yes, on assignment I met him. He decided to give his grandson a gift..."

"That don't sound too bad boss."

"It does when the gift was thirty-six dead bodies, including some friends, a fake mission and fifty trillion pounds that he wasn't supposed to have."

"Thirty-six dead bodies? That's the figure of fallen after the HQ attack."

"I know. It was the same event."

Finishing the drive in silent, Agent Dean noticed something wrong first.

"Sir, House Eight is missing."

"What?" Lewis looked at the house numbers; six, seven, nine, ten. The Manchez' lived at number eight. "Oh, crap. You're right."

Doing a tight 90° turn Agent Lewis hit his mic.

"YBD Hotel respond now!"
"This is YBD Hotel."

"Where the hell are you? And where's Manchez' house?"

"We're at Hotel D'Marcé, 227 West Moreland Avenue. House 8

was destroyed an hour ago as we left to go to the Hotel."

"Stay there! We're coming!"

Putting his foot down, ignoring the speed limit, the Humvee hit eighty on the long beachfront road. The tyres screamed as Agent Lewis turned a corner too tightly. The tire smoke was intoxicating as people looked in disgust at the huge 4x4. The Humvee ate the road, and petrol, as the small engine struggled to cope with the speed. One hundred miles an hour. The engine groaned and screamed as it tried to keep up. One ten. One fifteen. One twenty. One thirty. Zero.

The engine stalled as Lewis accidentally put the car in reverse from fifth, trying for sixth. The jolt hurt but the agents were trained to withstand worse pain.

Restarting the vehicle Lewis cursed his luck. A giant eighteen-wheeler were heading behind him beeping his horn.

Depressing the accelerator as hard as he could the engine

caught and sped away. Lewis barely saw another eighteen-wheeler coming in the wrong lane before it hit the front of the Humvee. With a sickening crunch, the front end crumpled into itself before destroying Lewis's body before the others. None of the Agents had had time to report the threat. All of them had felt light-headed right before the accident.

"Team Alpha, come in. Team Alpha. It is Director Green, YBD

Hotel are concerned. Where are you?"

Static.

"Agent Lewis, I swear to god, if this is a prank, you're fired!"

Static.

"Lewis? Anyone? Team Alpha report!" "Team Bravo come in." "We're here."

"Agent Lewis isn't responding. Any visuals?"

"No but reports are coming in about an armoured Humvee

being crushed by an eighteen wheeler going in the wrong direction. We are heading there to investigate as we speak."

"Negative, don't bother. I used LoJack (A tracking app/system installed in all of the GS Vehicles.). The Humvee was last on Route 8 towards Hotel D'Marcé. It must be them, head to the hotel, give YBD Hotel assistance. Over."

"Roger that."

Turning on his TV, Kyle saw a news report. It showed a Humvee destroyed with an eighteen-wheeler parked halfway through it. It looked like a gruesome hybrid vehicle.

"... We are told that there have been four casualties. All of them had strange ID cards on them. They appear to work for Greene Security based in the UK. Greene Security have been asked to come to identify these bodies. No driver has been found. The police are looking as hard as they can but it appears to be a horribly gruesome hit and run. Any witnesses are being urged to come forward."

Kyle switched off the TV. Cursing he looked at a picture frame on his desk. It including him and his team at graduation shortly after Alex had died and right before his Grandma had. He felt the tears rushing to his eyes. He let them pour down his face. He took off his headset and passed the mission update jobs to the Communications Department. The flow refused to let up as Kyle attempted to regain his composure before attempting to be Director again. He walked from his desk to the adjoining private bathroom. He rinsed his face and looked at his distorted, red reflection in the mirror. He had stopped crying now but he could still see the horrible looking mess of a hybrid vehicle gone wrong.

When he put the headset on the disconnected Comms from the channel as he began dealing with everything.

He heard gunshots and began panicking.

"Come in, come in!"

"Director it's Team Bravo, we arrived at the hotel and several gunmen came out of a parked petrol truck and began firing. For absolutely no reason! We are outnumbered but we are trying. I think the whole hotel has been taken over. There's been nothing from YBD Hotel, and Comms were really concerned."

"Okay, roger that, I'll try to do something from here, over."
"YBD Hotel come in, I repeat come in."

"This is Alexander Hopewell; hope your enjoying your fifty trillion pounds. You filthy…"

"You! How could you? This company was all you had. My father loved it; Grandma loved it, what happened?"

"Your dad saw too much so I had him killed. Your Grandma was injected fifteen years before her death, a month before mine, with a chemical that would cause heart attack symptoms but take fifteen years to take effect. If you had not become involved…

Maybe everything would have gone differently. You were *supposed* to be on-site during the attack."

That surprised Kyle.

"You wanted to kill me? Just for fifty trillion pounds? You are an animal. Good luck in the world, sir."

"Team Bravo? Get out of there. Team Hotel are gone. Principles are gone too. Come back home. Mission aborted."

His screen came alive with a red warning box. A nuclear missile was headed for the roof of their facility. It was an estimated twenty minutes away. He got up, changed all the access codes and ran to his bunker on the lowest level. He ordered all of his staff to join him. He was not going to have blood spilt on his hands unnecessarily.

Ten minutes later, everyone was in the bunker.

They all heard the impact as the missile destroyed everything in sight. They all felt the vibrations as the explosion ripped apart everything. They all felt the solemnness of the situation. They all thanked their lucky stars for the bunker. They all saw the dust shake from the girders. They all panicked. They all wished well for their families. They all thought they were going to die. They all felt relief as the doors opened and they saw extreme damage but a way out. They all cried as a firefighter ran across the dangerous debris to help. They all cried as more people began risking their lives climbing across the jungle of debris. They all cried into a shoulder. They all thanked everyone as they saw daylight. They all cursed the persons responsible. They all realised the high chance of being unemployed. They all saw the Director collapse. They all heard the ambulance arrive. They all saw the Ambulance crews shake their head. They all knew that Director Kyle Greene had somehow died, regardless of the missile. Moreover, they all felt regret that their saviour had died.

In addition, they all knew there was nothing they could do.

Two weeks later

Alexander Northumberland stood to attention outside the White House main entrance. It was a boring job most of the time. Stood next to him was Sarah Archero. Both belonged to the infamous Secret Service. At the gates, Agent Maximus radioed to let everyone know that a black

Rolls-Royce limousine had pulled up to the gates.

"Sir, welcome to the White House, I'm Agent Maximus. May I please see some ID and take your licence and registration?"

"Sure, Mr Maximus. I'm" he handed over the requested documents "Kyle Greene, Director of Greene Security LTD. I'd like to speak with President Columbus."

"I'm sure you do sir, just give me a second to scan these documents." He looked at his computer screen, surprised. He quickly masked the emotion and closed the privacy window.

"All Agents come in. We have a man called Kyle Greene here. Only problem is according to our systems he is deceased. As of two weeks ago."

"Ok, this is Senior Agent Northumberland. Let him in and I will speak to him. Meanwhile, Alpha Team prepare for standard evacuation procedures."

"Roger that, Agent Northumberland."

He reopened the privacy window and explained that before he could enter the White House he had to speak with Senior Agent Northumberland.

"Ok, that's fine, Mr Maximus, enjoy your day."

The limo driver waited until the gates had opened fully before driving forward. Turning around the Lincoln Fountain, the driver pulled up to the entrance where a suited man was waving.

"I'm Agent Northumberland. This is my colleague, Agent Archero. I hear you want to speak with the President?"

"That's right. I'm…"

"Kyle Greene, DOD two weeks ago. Can you explain this, please?"

"Easily. I… um… you are not exactly cleared for this information. Please can I speak with the President?"

"No, but I'll radio for Director Hopewell, maybe he can help."
"Director? We may have a

situation, can you please come down here. Main entrance, over."

Kyle could not hear the response but saw the giant seven-foot tall monstrosity of an agent. His deep voice was scary.

"Mr Greene? I thought you had died. Let him in Agent Northumberland."

"Yes, sir. Sorry Mr Greene."

The big oak doors opened silently. They walked silently towards the Oval Office.

"Kyle? You are alive! Thank heavens! We need Greene Security to undertake a mission as soon as..."

"I'm sorry to intrude Mr President, but Greene Security was destroyed in the missile attack."

"No, the HQ was. You and your team's determination is still very much alive. I have just one question. How are you alive?"

"Well, my official cause of death is smoke-inhalation-induced stroke. However, thanks to some new technology, Greene Securities, Scientific Development Department (The SDD) saved my life. They used Alpha Gel; it goes around a wound and closes it. Only problem was my wound was internal. So the needles built in popped out and injected the gel into my blood stream, closed my airways until I could have my stomach pumped to remove the smoke. However, publicly I would like to remain dead. I've decided that I will, with your blessing and assistance, become Arthur Walker, the new Director of

Walker Security, made using a sizeable donation from Greene Security."

"Of course, Kyle, of course. How soon can Walker Security become operational?"

"I have the new HQ underway. A ten billion pound complex. It will be finished tomorrow. The site was being made two years ago, when I inherited the business. I can take you on a tour the day after?"

"Sure, I'll be there, Director Walker." He smiled. "I like that name. It suits you perfectly."

"Thank you."

Arthur saluted and walked out of the office. He told his driver to take him to Ground 6, the codename of Walker HQ.

When he arrived, he saw his new Alpha Team assembled. There was Alex a tech geek, Sarah a Comms Expert, Tyler, Grace and Max were all operatives.

Alongside these was Dr Haranguer, a scientist specialising in technological and incognito devices. In front of all of these was his Security Team, a twelve person strong impregnable team.

"Welcome to Ground Six, Mr Walker. I am Security Director Lee Krieger. I oversee all security on this base. Your office is on the minus fifteenth floor. I'm sure you'll like it, sir."

"I am too, Director. Your team? I don't believe we've been acquainted."

"Oh of course! And we don't know these people here, we were about to get acquainted when you arrived."

"I'm Doctor Haranguer (Har-An-Ger); I'm in charge of the Scientific Development Department or the SDD." The doctor was in dress whites and had a receding grey hairline. He looked about fifty.

"I'm Alex the Geek, I'm in charge of the Technology Department." Alex was 19 and was dressed in jeans and a t-shirt.

"Sarah, I'm in charge of the Communications Department or Comms for short." Likewise, Sarah was 19 but she was dressed in black trousers and a white shirt.

"Tyler, Operative Alpha, I'm Team Leader of Alpha Team." Tyler was in his early twenties and had his tongue pierced. Dressed in a smart three-piece navy suit, he was one of the smartest dressed people there.

"Grace, I'm Operative Bravo, Second-In-Command." She was

eighteen and dressed in camouflage trousers and jacket.

"Maximus, Max though is what I go by, call me Maximus and I'll…"

"And your rank, Max?" Lee asked. "Oh, yeah. I am Operative Charlie. Just a regular agent."

"My security team have asked to be known only by tag, sir. I'll email you their details securely." "Very well, Lee. Right, all of you should know the President is coming for a tour the day after tomorrow. Nothing goes wrong, you hear me?"

"Yes Director Walker."

Arthur walked into the building where an open door revealed a chrome and gold elevator. He took it to minus fifteen. He saw his opulent office and gasped.

Two days later.

The large convoy left The White House at the same time. The twenty vehicle strong convoy sped across the highway towards Ground 6. Three choppers kept

the sky clear as they drove.
Everything was clear.

Outside Ground 6, four large armoured Chevrolet Suburbans stood side-by-side. All four belonged to the Secret Service Advance Team.

Ten miles from Ground 6 fifty large armoured, machine gun mounted Jeep Cherokees stood in five rows of ten. All fifty were jet black. All fifty had a logo of a green scorpion. There were five people in each car. Four inside and one on each gun. Everyone's radio crackled as the boss switched on his mic.

The Presidential Convoy took the turning for Ground 6 and everyone noticed the CCTV cameras every twenty or so feet.

"This is Boss. We are Mission Go. I repeat Mission Go. It's time for the Scorpions to eat the Ants!"

Silence

"This is Ground 6 Security. We have noted your approach, please identify yourselves."

The convoy's vehicles all had radios that received this message. Even the cameras said the message beside them.

The President keyed his mic.

"This is The President. May we approach?"
"Just one security question. What

is the birth name of our Director?"

"Kyle Greene."

"Affirmative. Continue. How many?"

"Twenty vehicles. Ten dignitaries."

"Roger. How many security?"

"Twenty. But when we arrive security goes to you."

"Roger. Out."

The first of the fifty Jeeps drove from its row and approached the access road.

"This is Private Land, turn around now! We have authorisation to shoot. Turn around now!" An automated voice screamed from the mics next to the vehicles. An alert was sent directly to Director Krieger.

The Director then saw the fifty cars driving up and swore.

"All teams to attack positions. I repeat all teams to their attack positions. Gate men, stick to normal professionalism. We do not want to panic our guests. Someone tell Director Walker, stat!"

"Roger that, sir."

A switch was used and three missile launchers rose from the towers surrounding the access gate to Ground 6.

They fired and hit the lead three vehicles. All three turned into black shells.

The launchers disappeared for five seconds as they reloaded.

One of the vehicles aimed a rocket at their missile launcher and fired. It broke with a giant smoke cloud. Two more rockets followed. Then one of the cars slammed into the gate. It did not budge. The sixteen tonne gate needed more than one off roader to break through. Apparently realizing their mistake, the rocket launcher reappeared and took aim. The rocket just dented the steel. Then ten cars lined up and pushed forward in a single-file line. As the first crashed into the dent, the second hit the rear of the first and so on. Soon there was a huge pile up as the ninth car went in. The gate strained as the tenth car pushed straight through. An eleventh broke the gate off entirely. Security were scared. They tried getting in contact with the convoy but nobody replied.

"Sir, we've got a big Blue-Alert situation going on." A robotic voice spoke to Director Walker.

"What is it?"
"Fifty enemies. Fifteen down. Ten

men down on our side. Convoy not responding. Last known location, five minutes away from Checkpoint One."

"Cancel all checkpoints. Get the President here and to the Bunker. Evacuate everyone but Security down there. Call Air Base Richardson, down the road and request back-up."

"All done. Back up is fifteen minutes away. Staff are evacuating now. Sleep Mode activated."

Arthur stood up. He pushed a button underneath his desk and all the beautiful pictures on his wall changed to CCTV feeds. The convoy was racing *away* from Ground 6 chased by about twenty vehicles. The sensors confirmed it. Twenty-one extra non-convoy vehicles. A machine gun rose from the first non-convoy vehicle and fired at the rear convoy vehicle. The car seemed to rise from the ground as five cars simultaneously fired at the same car. It then flipped onto the one in front of it. This happened until the convoy was destroyed. Then the vehicles turned around and headed for Ground 6. Seventy enemies would be too strong to fight off. They had to get to the Bunker. Quickly. Arthur grabbed his key card and sighed. A man stood at the entrance. He had entered as Arthur was watching the CCTV.

"Kyle." The man sounded familiar but Arthur could not place it,

"No I'm Arthur."

"You were born as Kyle Greene to my son."

"Grandfather. I have told you. Leave my companies and me alone. You proved your point, our security failed against numerous vehicles. It will be fixed, now please leave."

"I killed you. This time I won't fail." He pulled out a Sig Sauer. One of the Security weapons. He aimed at Arthurs head. "You're probably wearing armour. I am sorry it came to this. However, I need that money. Otherwise, I am dead. Deader than dead even. I have debts. I need to pay them."

"So you're going to kill me? How does that help you?"

"Simple, I own every charity and company around here. A bit like the Rockefellers. No matter where your pity existence goes, I'll end up with it." He shrugged. "I'm sure you won't mind."

"You are a horrible man. You should have died that day. Or at least had the decency to stay dead."

"Well, then it's a shame that you are the one with a gun a gun to your head."

A gun went off.

Chapter Two:

Seated at a large circular table the Cabinet sat discussing the recent destruction of Walker Security Head Quarters and the murder of President Columbus and other American Dignitaries. They all knew who the killer was. It was Fredrick Greene, Kyle Greene (and Arthur Walker's) grandfather. Somehow, he had infiltrated the HQ and destroyed the convoy that was heading there. Then, unbelievably, somebody had killed him. Nobody, not even Arthur knew who he or she were.

"Mr President, as General, I suggest that we initiate the Doomsday Protocols. Then we speak to Mr Walker about rebuilding his HQ. Then we re-evaluate our options from there."

"I agree, Mr President, this may be our only option. As Vice-President I vote for this option."

"Ladies, Gentlemen, I apologise. If you remember, only a handful of people knew about the Convoy and its exact location. One of these was Secret Service Agent Wilde, whom as you may remember is nowhere to be found. I have revoked their Secret Service privileges digitally. But," he sighed, "you're right, we should initiate Doomsday, and rebuild Walker Security HQ. Can we get a feed to him?"

"Of course, Mr President."

A three hundred inch screen descended from the ceiling and pixelated slightly as it connected to a smaller screen inside the Hospital Arthur was at.

"Mr Walker? Can you hear me?"

"Yes, President Hammer."

"Call me Chris. How soon can the HQ be rebuilt?"

"Sir, it was a disaster. I shouldn't be here," he signalled the hospital room, "I should be in prison. I killed several people with my lax security."

"Enough! You are wrong, Arthur. Your Grandfather is fully responsible! Now listen to me. I'm firing my entire Secret Service effective immediately"

"Mr President..."

"Be quiet General. I want to replace them with Walker Security Agents. Now, I ask again, how long?"
"Two months. Minimum. But"

"Ok, until then the Secret Service will remain. Now I have a suggestion to help us find your saviour. Do you agree to temporary hypnosis to see if your conscience remembers anything?"

"Sure, it's worth a try."

One **hour later.**

"Mr Walker, I want to take you back to the attack on Walker Security HQ. You are inside your office. A man is aiming a gun at you. That man is your grandfather. Now a man kills your grandfather, can you see who did it?"

"Yes."

"Can you describe them?"

"Blue suit, white earpiece. White shirt, gold tie. A green shield badge. Long black hair. Blue eyes. Female."

"Ok, thank you Mr Walker. Now what happens?"

"A man in a black suit runs in. He injects me with something."
"That was a sleep medication. You were stressed and faint. Can you describe the man?"

"I can do better; I know his name, Secret Service Agent Wilde."

"Oh, are you sure?"
"Sure about what?" Arthur had woken up at the emotion in the last question.

"You just described the killer perfectly. However, the man that injected you... It was not Agent Wilde. It was Agent King."

Three months later.

"I'm Simon Cole, and this is News Worldwide. We have a lot of news to tell you so stay tuned!"

"In breaking news a woman named Sarah Jacksonville has been named as Arthur Walker's saviour. The hunt for Agent Wilde has finally been concluded as they found him dead on site of the HQ as they finished rebuilding. Away from this sad news, fifteen million dollars was donated to Save the Animals earlier today. This sizeable donation was donated anonymously."

President Hammer switched off the news. He sighed. He had had to lie to the Media. Arthur had died of a heart attack in hospital a week earlier. This coincided with him meeting his saviour Sarah Jacksonville. President Hammer looked at his daily brief, supplied by his secretary. He had lunch with the Foreign Secretary in two hours. Other than that, he had nothing. His phone rang. The caller ID was withheld.

"Hello?"

"Mr President, my name is Miller, Jonathan Miller. I work for Special Operations at the Pentagon."

"OK, Mr Miller, continue."

"I just received orders from the Nuclear Football to release Nuke Zero, Zero, Seven, and One. Destination is the White House, can you confirm?"

President Hammer hung up quickly and ran down the hallway to the Oval Office. Sat at the desk was General O'Keefe. In front of him was the Nuclear Football, open.

"General? What are you doing?"

"What does it look like Mr President. You ordered the initiation of Doomsday. Yet look around! You're too weak to do anything. So I'm taking matters into my own hands."

"By blowing up the White House? How does that help?"

His phone rang again. A few seconds after the Generals did.

"President Hammer? It is Agent Miller, Special Ops, The Pentagon. The built-in Security confirmation feature was just overridden. The nuke just left. You have half an hour to get clear of Washington."

"What about the Public?"

"You're more important, sir, no offence to the people."

"Remove the Generals Access codes. Now."

"I need a confirmation code."
"Alpha, Bravo, Delta, Six, Six, Six, One, Zero, Yankee."

"Confirmed. New code sent to your PDA. General O'Keefe no longer has access to anything… What? The nuke just sent itself to space to self-destruct. Who sent the nuke?"

"The general. Send backup."
"On it."

The call ended. The General had visibly paled as the football closed itself and his access codes deleted themselves.

"Sir, I can explain…"
"Save it. I thought I could trust you. I was clearly wrong. I apologise for trusting you. Goodbye General."

Bang.

The President crumpled to the ground.

"No, I'm sorry, sir." He grabbed the Presidents PDA and looked at the access code. He entered the code into the keypad on the side of the football. The lid opened halfway.

"Please say your voice analysis code."
"What?"

"Incorrect. Please try again."

He grabbed the Presidents diary from his blazer pocket. His code was written down on the back page.

"Chestnuts and oak trees grow short."

"Correct... Access denied. Voice not recognised. Please try again."

Using a recording of one of the meetings and an app, he used his phone to recreate his voice saying the passphrase.

"Access granted."

The football opened fully. The LCD screen lit up. A cancel self-destruct button had appeared. He pushed it. The nuke continued on its original path to the White House. He lent back, satisfied.

Twenty minutes later

The nuke hit the dome at the centre of the White House. The explosion radiated outwards. The residents of Washington felt nothing as the toxic air entered their lungs, killing them instantly.

The country went into a state of high alert. Only one man knew the truth. And that man was in Virginia, at the Pentagon.

The A-Ring at the Pentagon was the most secure. Security stood at every corner. You could barely move twenty feet before you had your ID checked. Agent Miller had never felt so stressed before. When he finally arrived at the Vice-Generals office, he hesitated. *What if Vice-General Vicki Laker was involved?* He thought.

He knocked loudly.

"Enter."

He walked in.

"Ah, Agent Miller, I presume? Special Operations?"

"Yes, sir. I need to tell you something about the Washington situation."

"I know. Security told me you were coming. Something to do with General O'Keefe?"

"That's right sir. Permission to speak freely?"

"In the current situation how could I say no?"

"Well, ok. President Hammer's last order was to remove all access codes belonging to the General. Then, not ten minutes later, the nuke comes back online using the Presidents codes. But, get this; the football recognised *two* failed attempts."

"Ok, what's your point?"

"I think the General used the Presidents codes to get the nuke online."

"That's nonsense. Why would he sacrifice himself?"

"So that we don't suspect him. Sir, I understand that he is your boss. But..."

"I think you're right. There is no other explanation. I need to speak with Vice-President Trevor McGladys. We need to swear him in as President. I hereby, with no other choice, take office of the Vice-President. I vote you Agent Miller as General. Now sit down while I address the Vice-

President."
"Yes, sir."

A screen ascended from a dresser against the wall of the office.

"Vice-General, how can I help?"
"I am afraid that in light of the recent attack on the White House, we need to swear you in. Due to my bosses office now being vacant I take the seat, however, with you taking office of President, I will have to take the promotion to Vice-President. This is Special Agent Miller, from Special Operations, he was in

charge of SO. He will be promoted to General, unless, of course, you object?"

"Of course not. Should I head to the Pentagon?"

"Yes, if you can. Until further notice, Emergency Delta Six, Six One will be initiated. Again, unless you object?"

"Go ahead. Listen. I think..."

The feed cut out to fuzz as the connection was lost. The Vice-General keyed a mic on his desk.

"Air Force Two, come in. Air Force Two."

"This is Air Force Two. We have a mayday, I repeat, we have a mayday. Left engine failure. Jesus! Whole engine failure! I repeat whole engine failure. Oh, dear god, no. Total systems collapse. I repeat total systems..."

The plane's systems beeped once before stopping. The loss of power resulted in the sixty two thousand tonne plane in dropping rapidly. The pilots battled the controls as much as they could. Then an LCD screen lit up.

"Engine reboot. Systems reboot. In progress. Sixty percent complete." The calm female voice came through a tannoy above the pilots' heads. They looked at each other.

"Reboots complete. Seventy percent power. Fuel at seventeen percent. Refuel within five hundred miles. Autopilot engaged by P-Gen O'Keefe. Resuming path to the Pentagon. Communications systems shutting down. Shut down." The calm voice had just shut the pilots off from their own aircraft. Both tried as hard as they could to regain control. Finally, the plane dipped low enough for Pilot Granger to get phone reception. He dialled the Pentagons Internal line.

Vice-General Laker answered calmly.

"Hello, The Pentagon, A-Ring, VG Laker speaking."
"This is Pilot Granger, Air Force Two. We have a problem."

OPERATION NIGHTSHADE

CLASSIFIED MATERIAL

DO NOT COPY

DO NOT MAKE NOTES

FOR PRESIDENTIAL EYES ONLY

COMMS ACCESS DENIED

This is a mission memorandum supplied by GENERAL O'KEEFE. Dictated to HOPEWELL, SARAH

ORIGINAL DOCUMENT.

AIM: COMPLETE MISSION SUCCESSFULLY

OBJECTIVES IN ORDER OF NECCESSITY;

FAKE PRESIDENTIAL DEATH

KILL VICE-GENERAL, VICE-PRESIDENT

- KILL KYLE GREENE/ARTHUR WALKER
- SEND NUCLEAR WEAPON TO WHITE HOUSE
- FAKE GENERALS DEATH
- SEND AIR FORCE TWO TO PENTAGON
- KILL ALL RESIDENTS OF WASHINGTON
- USE ARMOURED P-14 TANKS
- ATTACK ANDREWS AIR BASE
- DESTROY ANDREWS AIR BASE

DESTROY AIR FORCE ONE

DESTROY ALL GROUND AND WATER FORCE VEHICLES

Signed by: *General O'Keefe*

Co-signed by: *Sarah Hopewell*

Witnessed by: Holly Simmons-Fraiser

General O'Keefe looked at his memo. Sat next to him was President Hammer. In front of him was a contract

I, PRESIDENT HAMMER, AGREE TO FOLLOW THE MEMO, AND ALL ORDERS FROM WITHIN, TO MY BESTEST ABILITY REGARDLESS OF ALL IMPLICATIONS AND VIEWPOINTS OF THE PUBLIC, MEDIA AND ANY OTHER SOURCE OF OPINION.

SIGNED: *General O'Keefe*

SIGNED: _____

"Well, Mr President? Sign the document."

"No, I can't. If I do, I'll label myself as a terrorist."

"Oh, really? That is a shame, Mr President. Now sign the goddam document before I kill your son."

Sat next to the General was the President's son, Alexander Hammer.

President Hammer picked up the biro. He looked at the small piece of white paper in front of him. He looked at his son.

"Stop stalling. Sign."

He looked back at the paper. He put the pen to paper. He signed. The General picked up the paper before he could change his mind.

"Good. Now" he pulled out a Sig Sauer and fired a single supressed bullet into Alexander's forehead. He then turned the gun around and aimed it at the shell-shocked President. He fired another supressed bullet into the Presidents forehead.

General O'Keefe walked away. At the end of the forest he had been in was a bus stop. The first bus that arrived, he boarded. Two hours later, he arrived in Michigan. He went to a Post Office and got an envelope and stamp so that he could send the contract and memorandum to the Pentagon. They would read this on their way to a bunker, after reading about the destruction of all the important buildings.

Two days later

In the F-Ring of the Pentagon, a postal officer arrived with a letter addressed as urgent.

Checking it in all of the scanners the contents were deemed safe. Security Officer James Sawyer called the Vice General and asked him to collect the letter.

After reading the document, he arranged an Emergency Meeting.

"Now we have no idea who this letter was sent by but according to both of these legalised documents President Hammer and General O'Keefe had arranged a mission to destroy all our government buildings and fake each other's deaths. This is important. Somebody in the Tracking Department also noticed something strange. President Hammer's son, Alexander has not been seen since the first attack. We believe that this is key to

figuring out what is going..."
"Sir, sorry to interrupt but we've just found President Hammer and his son. They've been murdered."

"General O'Keefe?"
"No location. Possibly the murderer."

"Thank you, Agent. Close the door behind you."

The man left.

"I now think I know who sent this letter. General O'Keefe. As a precaution, we will remain here.

He probably wants us to evacuate.

In Michigan General O'Keefe dialled his desk.

"This is the voicemail for General O'Keefe. Leave a message and I definitely won't listen to it."

"This is O'Keefe."

"This is Vice General Laker. Where in hell are you?"

"Michigan. I need a pickup. Some mad person tried killing me. He kidnapped the President, his son, and me. Then he tried killing all three of us. I tried to save them but..."

"We received the letter, General. We are staying at the Pentagon. Now listen very carefully to me. We have reviewed CCTV of the White House on our records here at the Pentagon. We have no sightings of an enemy. Your story is total bull and you know it. The only pickup you'll be getting is the Prison Bus."

"Now listen to me! I have no doubt that you disbelieve me but I swear on my daughter's life that I'm telling the truth."

"Your *daughter*?"

"Yes I have a daughter. She is 20 and lives in Washington. 17 Whitaker Drive. 20013. She will be there. Talk to her."

"We will. Look, I believe you. I *know* you would not do anything to harm the First Family. I'll see what I can do."

"Thank you."

The Vice-General hung up.

In the Pentagon, Agent Baker had just arrived with Sarah Jacksonville, Agent Greene's saviour and, apparently, General O'Keefe's adult daughter.

"Ms Jacksonville. Last time we spoke, it was about medals. This time…"
"I know Vice-General, it's about my dad. He…" she began crying "is a… good man. He wouldn't hurt a fly…"

"I know." Vice General O'Keefe replied walking over and embracing her "But he is also a two faced traitor. We just received word that Air Force Two just crashed into Andrews Air Base, destroying most of the aerial vehicles kept there. We also found records that it was your dads' mobile phone that hacked into Air Force Twos' systems."

"What? How sure are you?" she had stopped crying and looked into the VG's eyes.

"I'm afraid we can't be surer." He looked at Agent Baker "we'll take her with us. Less chance of an attack.

Agent Baker pulled his gun

"What are you doing Agent?" Laker demanded.

"What I should have done a long time ago." He fired a bullet into Lakers forehead.

He collapsed to the floor, dead.

"Now, Ms Jacksonville. Let's go to Manor D'Kingston as requested by Mr O'Keefe. We'll take a Security Convoy."

"I refuse. My father is an awful man. He killed many people. I cannot forget that."

"That man" he signalled the dead body "is a liar. Your father would do nothing to harm anyone."

"Or would he? I do not think I knew my father as much as I thought I did. I just need some time."

"We don't have that luxury anymore. Any second now,

somebody will try ringing the Vice-General and they will realise that he has been murdered. Then we are both screwed. Now let us go. You can have the time in the car."

"No. You go alone."

"Fine" he put his gun away. Then he pulled out a Taser and aimed it at her chest. She collapsed into a heap on the floor by his feet. He grabbed her and put her over his shoulder. Just as he did this, a piercing alarm went off.

"Damn it!"

He ran out of the office with Sarah slung over his shoulder. Gun out he, felt invincible as he ran towards the exit. Nobody questioned him as he ran.

The glass doors swung open as he ran towards them. Outside a silver Volkswagen Golf sat idling. It was armoured with run-flats and tinted windows. Plan 1 was a fail so he threw Sarah onto the back seat and got in the front. The tires span as they tried to gain purchase on the ground. Then he heard a clang and understood what had happened. Somebody had put a clamp on the wheel.

"Agent Baker. Where are you going? We need to talk." Agent Miller from Special Operations stood outside the vehicle with four security officers. "Now why don't you go and throw the gun away?"

Printed in Great
Britain
by Amazon